Melena's Jubilee

Tilbury House Publishers
Thomaston, Maine

Melena's Jubilee

The Story of a Fresh Start

Zetta Elliott

illustrated by Aaron Boyd

I woke up this morning with a song
in my heart and looked out my window.

The night rain had washed away
our chalk drawings, but I didn't mind.
The sidewalk was clean,
and that meant we could start over.

This morning I remembered to make my bed.

Yesterday I forgot.

Yesterday I also forgot to put my toys away, and when Gramma's friend came over, he tripped on one and banged into the table.

That's how my mother's favorite vase got broken.

It seemed like everyone was mad at me.

This morning when I crept into the kitchen and slipped into my seat, Gramma winked at me. Mama set down my breakfast and kissed the top of my head.

"Does this mean you aren't mad at me anymore?" I asked them.

"I never let the sun go down on my anger," Gramma said.

"Today's a new day, Melena," Mama added, "and that means you've got a fresh start. After work I'm going to stop at the store to get some glue. Maybe this evening you can help me fix my vase."

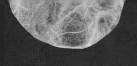

After breakfast I told Gramma about the song in my heart. She put the dishes in the sink and began running the water. Steam and bubbles drifted up towards my grandmother's pretty face.

"I feel that way some days," she said. "Some days I wake up feeling like I'm brand new."

She chuckled. "And that's a pretty special feeling for an old lady like me!"

I chuckled, too, and told Gramma that today felt like the first page of a brand-new book.

"Well, what are you planning to write on that first page?" she asked me.

I told her I wasn't sure.

When we finished the dishes, I called my best friend Helen and told her to meet me outside. On my way out, I passed behind my older brother Miles. I thought about the time last week when he snuck up behind me and whacked me over the head with his tennis racquet.

Now I had a chance to pay him back.

I thought about how surprised Miles would be when the heavy cushion from the sofa went WHUMP! upside his head.

But then I remembered that this was my Fresh Start Day, and pounding Miles didn't seem like such a good idea. After all, he'd only hit me back, and Miles hits hard.

So I left him alone and went outside.

Helen was standing on the sidewalk. She looked upset.

"What's wrong?" I asked.

"The poem I wrote about the rainbow got washed away," said Helen.

"So write a new poem," I suggested.

Helen knelt down and started drawing a flower instead. I took a piece of chalk and wrote, "There is a song in my heart."

"What's your song about?" Helen asked.

"I'm not sure," I said, "but it makes me want to celebrate."

Helen stopped drawing. "Celebrate what?"

I looked around. "I don't know. Maybe the sun, or those trees over there. We could celebrate flowers and birds—we could even celebrate being friends!"

Helen rolled her eyes. "Whatever you say, Melena."

I hummed softly to myself.

When it was time for lunch, we went inside.

"Gramma's out back," Miles mumbled with his mouth full of food.

Helen and I looked out the back door and saw Gramma digging in her garden. "Are you girls hungry?" she called to us.

Helen and I nodded.

Suddenly I had an idea. "Gramma, why don't we eat the things that are growing in your garden?"

Gramma pushed back her sunhat and studied me for a minute. Then she shrugged, picked up her basket, and started telling us what to pick.

We had the most delicious lunch!

When we finished eating, Gramma gave us some money. Helen and I ran outside and followed the tinkling tune of the ice cream truck. Up the block we saw Gavin and his twin brothers.

Helen tugged my arm. "Hey, Mel—Gavin owes you a dollar, remember?"

I remembered. I loaned it to him last week at the pizza shop. Gavin never gets to buy anything for himself. He always has to share with his little brothers.

When we reached the truck, Helen tugged my arm again. "Tell Gavin you want your money back," she whispered. "Then we can get double-swirl cones!"

Gavin was counting coins in the palm of his hand. He looked up and smiled at us.

"Hey, Melena. Hey, Helen."

On any other day, I would have told Gavin I wanted my money back. But today was my Fresh Start Day.

"Let's pool our money," I suggested.

"That way we can buy a hot fudge sundae and split it five ways."

"Five ways?!" gasped Helen.

The twins started jumping up and down.

"Sprinkles! Sprinkles!" they cried.

Gavin stared at the coins in his hand.

"I'm not sure, Melena...."

"Well, I am," I said.

We carried our hot fudge sundae over to the park and dug in. Then we spread out on top of the jungle gym and took turns pointing out funny-shaped clouds.

After a while we got quiet.

Then Gavin said, "Have you ever thought about the sun?"

"What about it?" I asked.

"Well," said Gavin, "there's only one. One sun that shines on everybody in the world, no matter where you live or how you look or how much money you have."

"Sunshine's free for everyone," said Helen.

"I never thought of it that way," I said.

We got quiet again.

I closed my eyes and felt
the sun beaming down on
me. I began to hum, softly
at first, but Gavin heard
me and joined in.

"Is that the song in your heart?"
asked Helen.

I nodded and kept on humming.

"What's it about?" asked Gavin.

"Oh, lots of things," I said. "It's
about waking up to a blue sky and
finding out you've been forgiven.
It's about free sunshine, and
the tasty things that grow in my
grandmother's garden. But mostly
it's about having a chance to start
all over again, every single day!"

Author's Note

For this story, I used the concept of jubilee to represent Melena's fresh start. She is forgiven by her family after making a mistake, and Melena doesn't make Gavin pay back the money she loaned him. On this otherwise ordinary day Melena tries to do things differently, and the song in her heart fills her with joy and peace.

Jubilee has long held a special place in the hearts of African Americans. Enslaved Africans had their own religions when they were brought to the Americas, but African Americans embraced Christianity over time. Although most slaves were forbidden from learning to read, Bible stories were shared orally, and some enslaved people memorized the verses that gave them comfort. The practice of jubilee is explained in the Book of Leviticus: every 50 years, slaves were to be freed, debts forgiven, and families reunited. Not surprisingly, jubilee held special meaning for enslaved African Americans who longed for freedom and the chance to be with their loved ones. When President Lincoln signed the Emancipation Proclamation on January 1, 1863, African Americans declared it the Day of Jubilee. The proclamation only freed slaves in those states that had seceded from the Union, but African Americans believed the president's gesture signaled the end of slavery. Jubilee Day continues to be celebrated in some parts of the country, and serves as an opportunity for African Americans to reflect on the past and focus on ways to strengthen their communities.

We don't have to wait 50 years to do things that can change our lives and improve our communities. Every day when we wake up we can choose not to hold onto anger or fight with others—we can choose instead to see the beauty in our world and share what we have with those in need.

The spirit of jubilee also lives on in the global campaign for debt relief. Many social justice activists believe that impoverished countries shouldn't be forced to repay loans from wealthy countries—especially when the unfair extraction of resources by the creditor countries created that poverty in the first place. When debt is forgiven, millions of dollars can go toward better schools, hospitals, and roads. Lifting the burden of debt from poor countries can enable them to grow their economies and become independent so that loans aren't needed in the future.

Jubilee remains relevant in our world because everyone understands the value of starting over.

Here are seven things you can do to have your very own "fresh start day!"

1. Make a clean sweep! Tidy your room and donate to charity any unused toys or clothes you no longer wear.

2. Give back! Return items you've borrowed from others, including overdue library books.

3. Pay it back and pay it forward! Pay back any money you owe to others, including outstanding fines at the library. If you have a little extra, share what you have with others: donate canned goods to a food bank or volunteer to help out at your local soup kitchen or nonprofit.

4. Make the most of what you have! Throw a party, prepare a meal, or dress for a special occasion without going to the store to buy something new.

5. Do something nice for others—just because! You don't have to wait for a holiday or birthday to make someone in your life feel special. Think about something a loved one needs, and give it without expecting anything in return. You don't have to spend any money— you can write a poem, share a good joke, or send a letter filled with encouraging words! Doing someone else's chores without being asked can also give that person time to relax, and time is a precious gift.

6. Choose peace! When someone upsets you, don't respond with anger. Walk away or pay that person a compliment instead.

7. Try smiling at everyone you meet for the entire day, even if they don't smile back. Choose to stay positive and show kindness to others without expecting to be thanked.

Tilbury House Publishers
12 Starr Street
Thomaston, Maine 04861
800-582-1899 • www.tilburyhouse.com

Hardcover ISBN 978-088448-443-1
eBook ISBN 978-9-88448-445-5

First hardcover printing October 2016

15 16 17 18 19 20 XXX 10 9 8 7 6 5 4 3 2 1

Library of Congress Control Number: 2016945979

Designed by Kathy Squires

Printed in China through Four Colour Print Group, Louisville, KY
7/18/2016
Printed by Shenzhen Caimei, Shenzhen, China
67474-0

Born in Canada, Zetta Elliott moved to the U.S. in 1994 to pursue her PhD in American Studies at NYU. Her poetry has been published in several anthologies, and her plays have been staged in New York, Chicago, and Cleveland. Her essays have appeared in *The Huffington Post, School Library Journal,* and *Publishers Weekly.* She is the author of more than twenty books for young readers, including the award-winning picture book *Bird.* Her urban fantasy novel *Ship of Souls* was named a *Booklist* Top Ten Sci-fi/Fantasy Title for Youth. Three books published under her own imprint, Rosetta Press, have been named Best Children's Books of the Year by the Bank Street Center for Children's Literature. Elliott is an advocate for greater diversity and equity in publishing.

Aaron Boyd is the illustrator of 25 children's books including *Luigi and the Barefoot Races, Babu's Song, Daddy Goes to Work,* and the *Panda Goes to School* series. His pop-up Storybook Year won a Clio Top 4 award and was inducted into the Smithsonian Rare Books collection. He has also received Children's Africana Book, Choices Sports, Notable Children's Book, and Hermes Creative awards, and his advertising graphics have received Addy Gold and Graphis awards.